EL HOMBRE DE LA MÁSCARA PLATEADA

EL GALLO ENMASCARADO

EL TORO GRANDE

LUCHA LIBRE:
★ THE MAN IN THE ★
SILVER MASK

A BILINGUAL CUENTO

WRITTEN & ILLUSTRATED BY XAVIER GARZA

EL CUCUY

EL VAMPIRO

EL CAVERNICOLA

★ ★ ★ ★ ★ ★ ★ ★ ★ ★ ★ ★ ★ ★

"¡MÁSCARAS! COMPREN SUS MÁSCARAS! Get your

souvenirs right here," hollers the man selling lucha libre masks and souvenirs.

The bus has just dropped my Papá Lupe and me off at the arena. Papá Lupe had promised to take me to see lucha libre the next time we went to visit my Tío Vicente in Mexico City, and now we're here. But my Tío Vicente isn't anywhere around.

"Why didn't Tío Vicente come with us?" I ask Papá Lupe. "Doesn't he like lucha libre?"

"Your uncle LOVES lucha libre," answers Papá Lupe. "And you're going to love lucha libre too, Carlitos. You'll think your comic book superheroes have come to life!

★ ★ ★ ★ ★ ★ ★ ★

★ ★ ★ ★ ★ ★ ★ ★ ★ ★ ★ ★ ★ ★ ★ ★

—¡MÁSCARAS! ¡COMPREN SUS MÁSCARAS! Compren aquí sus recuerdos —grita el hombre que vende recuerdos y máscaras de lucha libre.

El camión nos acaba de dejar junto a la arena. Papá Lupe había prometido llevarme a la lucha libre la próxima vez que visitáramos a mi tío Vicente en la ciudad de México, y ahora ya estamos ahí. Pero mi tío Vicente no aparece.

—¿Por qué no vino el tío Vicente con nosotros? —le pregunto a Papá Lupe— ¿No le gustan las luchas?

—A tu tío le encanta la lucha libre —contesta papá Lupe—. Y a ti también te va a encantar. ¡Es como si cobraran vida los superhéroes de tus comics!

★ ★ ★ ★ ★ ★ ★ ★ ★ ★ ★ ★ ★ ★ ★ ★

★ ★ ★ ★ ★ ★ ★ ★ ★ ★ ★ ★ ★ ★ ★ ★ ★ ★

"ARE MEXICAN WRESTLERS REALLY superheroes?" I ask.

"They are better than superheroes, mi'jo," Papá Lupe assures me. "Luchadores are real people who nobody ever sees without their masks!"

"Wow," I say. "Then anybody could be a masked luchador, right?"

"That's right," Papá Lupe says. "Anybody —and I mean anybody—could be a masked luchador and you would never even know it."

★ ★ ★ ★ ★ ★ ★ ★ ★ ★ ★ ★ ★ ★ ★ ★ ★ ★

★ ★ ★ ★ ★ ★ ★ ★ ★ ★ ★ ★ ★ ★ ★ ★ ★

—¿DE VERAS SON SUPER-
HÉROES los luchadores mexicanos?
—le pregunto.

   —Son mejor que los superhéroes, mi'jo
—me asegura Papá Lupe—. ¡Los luchadores son
personas que nadie ha visto sin sus máscaras!

   —Órale. Entonces cualquier persona
podría ser un luchador enmascarado, ¿verdad?

   —Así es —dice Papá Lupe—, cualquier
persona podría ser un luchador y nosotros no
lo sabríamos.

★ ★ ★ ★ ★ ★ ★ ★ ★ ★ ★ ★ ★ ★ ★ ★ ★

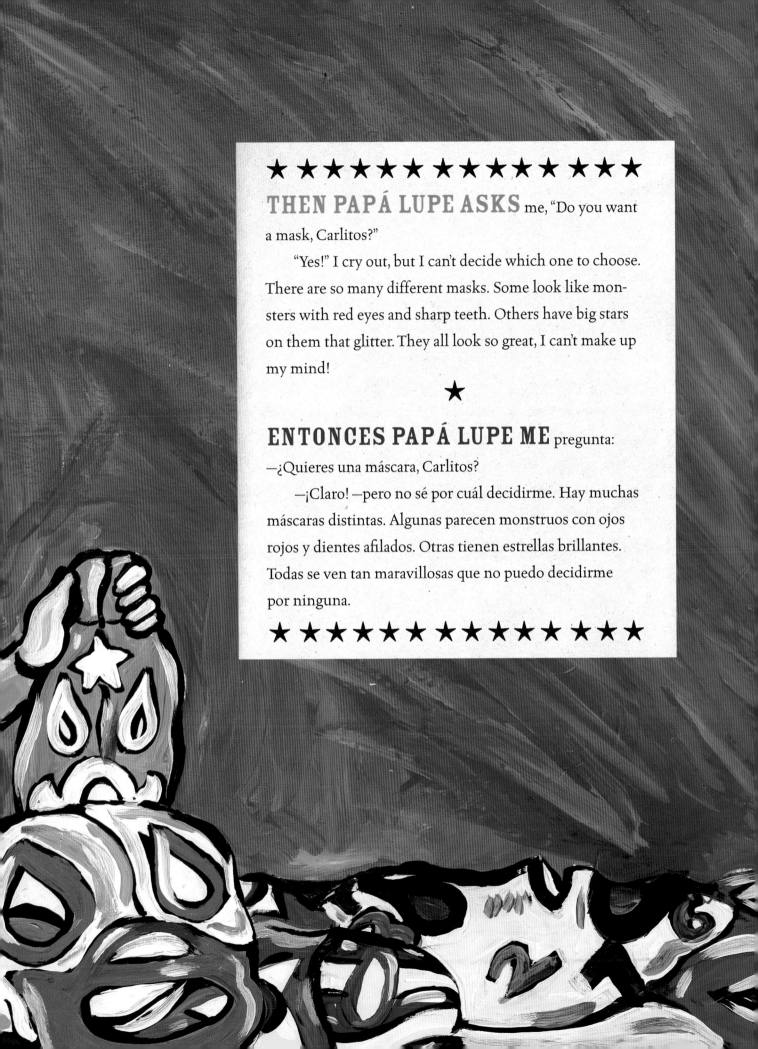

★ ★ ★ ★ ★ ★ ★ ★ ★ ★ ★ ★ ★ ★ ★

THEN PAPÁ LUPE ASKS me, "Do you want a mask, Carlitos?"

"Yes!" I cry out, but I can't decide which one to choose. There are so many different masks. Some look like monsters with red eyes and sharp teeth. Others have big stars on them that glitter. They all look so great, I can't make up my mind!

★

ENTONCES PAPÁ LUPE ME pregunta:
—¿Quieres una máscara, Carlitos?

—¡Claro! —pero no sé por cuál decidirme. Hay muchas máscaras distintas. Algunas parecen monstruos con ojos rojos y dientes afilados. Otras tienen estrellas brillantes. Todas se ven tan maravillosas que no puedo decidirme por ninguna.

★ ★ ★ ★ ★ ★ ★ ★ ★ ★ ★ ★ ★ ★ ★

★ ★ ★ ★ ★ ★ ★ ★ ★ ★ ★ ★ ★ ★ ★ ★ ★ ★

"YOU BETTER HURRY UP and pick one, mi'jo," says Papá Lupe. "I think the show is going to start."

"I want that one!" I point to a shiny silver mask with cutout silhouettes for its eyes, nose and mouth.

"Your boy has good taste, señor!" declares the man. "He has chosen The Man in the Silver Mask. He is the greatest luchador of all time!"

Papá Lupe smiles. I know he is proud of my decision.

★

—MÁS VALE QUE TE APURES y escojas una, mi'jo —dice Papá Lupe—. Parece que va a empezar.

—¡Quiero esa! —una brillante máscara plateada con siluetas recortadas para los ojos, la nariz y la boca.

—Su niño tiene buen gusto, señor —dice el vendedor—. Escogió la de El Hombre de la Máscara Plateada. ¡Es el más grande luchador de todos los tiempos!

Papá Lupe sonríe. Sé que está orgulloso de mi decisión.

★ ★ ★ ★ ★ ★ ★ ★ ★ ★ ★ ★ ★ ★ ★ ★ ★ ★

★ ★ ★ ★ ★ ★ ★ ★ ★ ★ ★ ★ ★ ★ ★ ★

THEN WE ARE SITTING at ringside.

"I sure wish Tío Vicente was here," I tell Papá Lupe.

"Tío Vicente is a funny sort of guy," says Papá Lupe.

"He might show up when you least expect it."

★

NOS SENTAMOS EN LA primera fila.

—Me gustaría que mi tío Vicente estuviera aquí —
le digo a Papá Lupe.

—Uno nunca sabe con tu tío Vicente —contesta—.
Podría aparecerse por aquí en cualquier momento.

★ ★ ★ ★ ★ ★ ★ ★ ★ ★ ★ ★ ★ ★ ★ ★

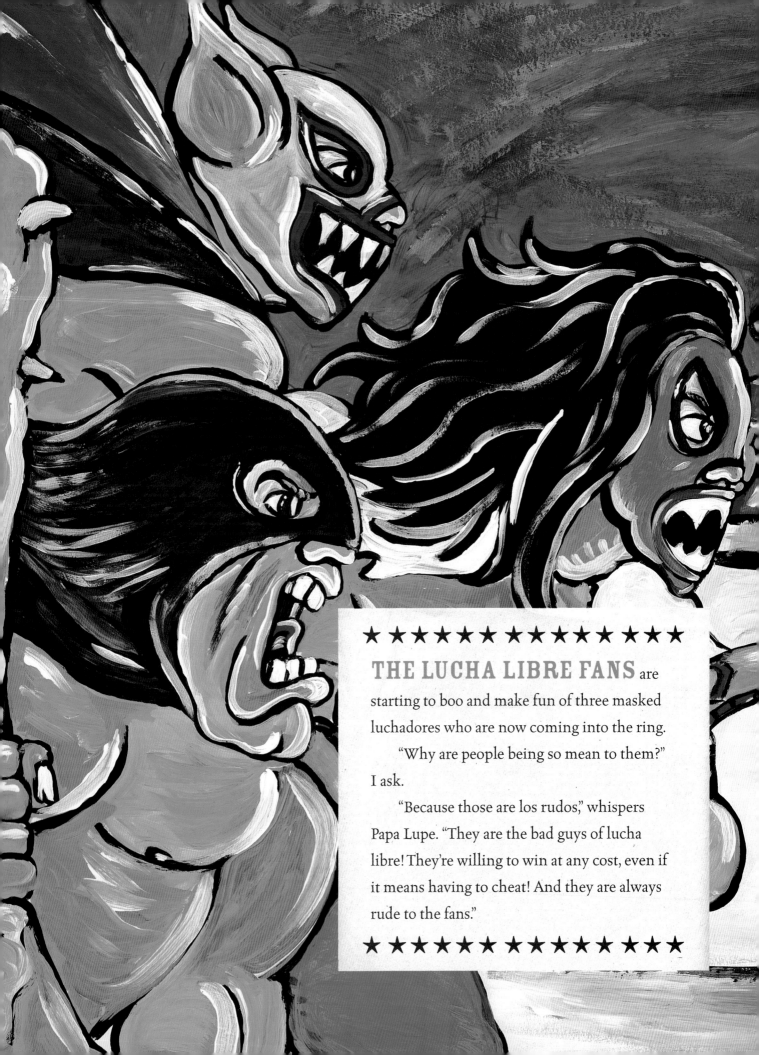

★ ★ ★ ★ ★ ★ ★ ★ ★ ★ ★ ★ ★ ★ ★ ★ ★

THE LUCHA LIBRE FANS are starting to boo and make fun of three masked luchadores who are now coming into the ring.

"Why are people being so mean to them?" I ask.

"Because those are los rudos," whispers Papa Lupe. "They are the bad guys of lucha libre! They're willing to win at any cost, even if it means having to cheat! And they are always rude to the fans."

★ ★ ★ ★ ★ ★ ★ ★ ★ ★ ★ ★ ★ ★ ★ ★ ★

★ ★ ★ ★ ★ ★ ★ ★ ★ ★ ★ ★ ★ ★

LOS FANÁTICOS DE LA LUCHA libre empiezan a abuchear y burlarse de tres enmascarados que se suben al ring.

—¿Por qué la gente es tan mala con ellos?

—Porque son rudos —me dice bajito Papá Lupe—. Son los malos de las luchas. Están dispuestos a ganar a cualquier precio. ¡Son unos tramposos! Y esos luchadores son muy groseros con el público.

★ ★ ★ ★ ★ ★ ★ ★ ★ ★ ★ ★ ★ ★

★ ★ ★ ★ ★ ★ ★ ★ ★ ★ ★ ★ ★ ★ ★ ★ ★ ★ ★ ★

EL CUCUY IS THE first rudo to enter the ring. His face is hidden by a green mask. His mouth is full of fanged white teeth like a great white shark. He's so scary that he makes me shake all over! He's wearing green tights and a white cape that looks like a torn rag wrapped around his thick neck. He walks around the ring barefoot and makes snorting and growling sounds as if he were a wild beast. I don't want him to come near me!

★ ★ ★ ★ ★ ★ ★ ★ ★ ★ ★ ★ ★ ★ ★ ★ ★ ★ ★ ★

★ ★ ★ ★ ★ ★ ★ ★ ★ ★ ★ ★ ★ ★ ★ ★ ★

EL CUCUY ES EL primer rudo que sube al ring. Su cara está oculta con una máscara verde. Su boca está llena de filosos dientes, como los de un tiburón blanco. ¡Es tan horrible que me hace temblar! Usa un leotardo verde y alrededor del cuello una capa blanca que parece un trapo roto. No trae zapatos y anda bufando y rugiendo como si fuera un animal salvaje. ¡No quiero que se me acerque!

★ ★ ★ ★ ★ ★ ★ ★ ★ ★ ★ ★ ★ ★ ★ ★ ★

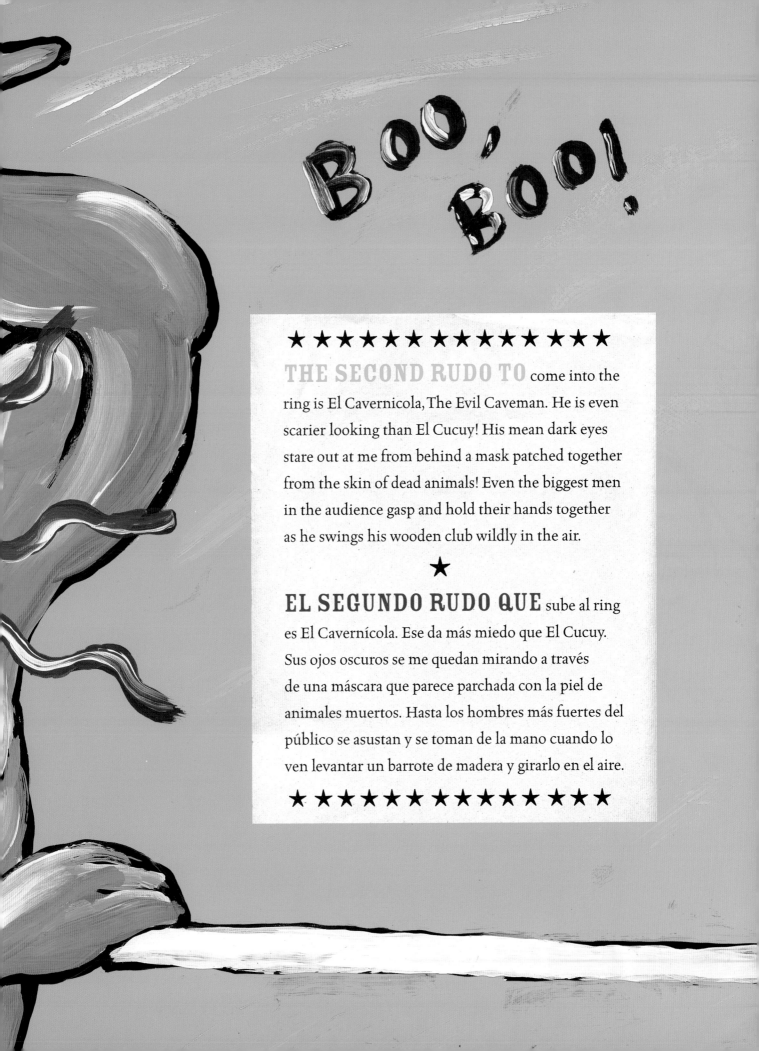

Boo, Boo!

★ ★ ★ ★ ★ ★ ★ ★ ★ ★ ★ ★ ★ ★ ★ ★

THE SECOND RUDO TO come into the ring is El Cavernicola, The Evil Caveman. He is even scarier looking than El Cucuy! His mean dark eyes stare out at me from behind a mask patched together from the skin of dead animals! Even the biggest men in the audience gasp and hold their hands together as he swings his wooden club wildly in the air.

★

EL SEGUNDO RUDO QUE sube al ring es El Cavernícola. Ese da más miedo que El Cucuy. Sus ojos oscuros se me quedan mirando a través de una máscara que parece parchada con la piel de animales muertos. Hasta los hombres más fuertes del público se asustan y se toman de la mano cuando lo ven levantar un barrote de madera y girarlo en el aire.

★ ★ ★ ★ ★ ★ ★ ★ ★ ★ ★ ★ ★ ★ ★ ★

★ ★ ★ ★ ★ ★ ★ ★ ★ ★ ★ ★ ★ ★ ★ ★ ★ ★

THE THIRD RUDO IS wearing a gray cape that look like the leathery wings of a vampire bat. Even his mask looks like the giant head of a bat. He is El Vampiro, a genuine living vampire who feeds on blood. At least, that's what the ring announcer says.

★ ★ ★ ★ ★ ★ ★ ★ ★ ★ ★ ★ ★ ★ ★ ★

EL TERCER RUDO USA una capa gris como las alas de un vampiro. Hasta su máscara parece la cabeza gigante de un murciélago. Es El Vampiro, un vampiro de verdad que bebe sangre humana. Al menos, eso es lo que dice el señor que anuncia a los luchadores.

★ ★ ★ ★ ★ ★ ★ ★ ★ ★ ★ ★ ★ ★ ★ ★

"LOS TÉCNICOS ARE NEXT!"

yells Papá Lupe.

"What's a técnico?" I ask.

"Los técnicos are the good guys! A true técnico will never cheat to win in any of his matches. He'll always earn his victory fair and square by using his superior wrestling skills. Fans love the técnicos, and will cheer for them as long and hard as they will boo for the rudos!

★ ★ ★ ★ ★ ★ ★ ★ ★ ★ ★ ★ ★ ★ ★ ★

★ ★ ★ ★ ★ ★ ★ ★ ★ ★ ★ ★ ★ ★ ★ ★

—SIGUEN LOS TÉCNICOS —

grita Papá Lupe.

—¿Qué son técnicos? —le pregunto.

—¡Los técnicos son los buenos! Un técnico de verdad nunca hace chapuza para ganar. Siempre gana por sus habilidades de luchador, sin hacer trampa. La gente adora a los técnicos y les echa porras con tanta fuerza como abuchea a los rudos.

★ ★ ★ ★ ★ ★ ★ ★ ★ ★ ★ ★ ★ ★ ★ ★

★ ★ ★ ★ ★ ★ ★ ★ ★ ★ ★ ★ ★ ★ ★ ★ ★

EL TORO GRANDE, The Mighty Bull, is the first técnico to step into the ring. He is very tall. He wears a mask with two large horns that point out from his forehead like a bull's!

"El Toro Grande sure looks strong," I tell my Papá Lupe.

"He is strong, as strong as a real bull! His arms are five times as big as mine!"

★

EL TORO GRANDE ES el primer técnico que sube al ring. Es muy alto. Usa una máscara con dos grandes cuernos que salen de su frente como los de un toro.

—El Toro Grande se ve muy fuerte —le digo a Papá Lupe.

—Es tan fuerte como un toro verdadero. Sus brazos son cinco veces más anchos que los míos.

★ ★ ★ ★ ★ ★ ★ ★ ★ ★ ★ ★ ★ ★ ★ ★

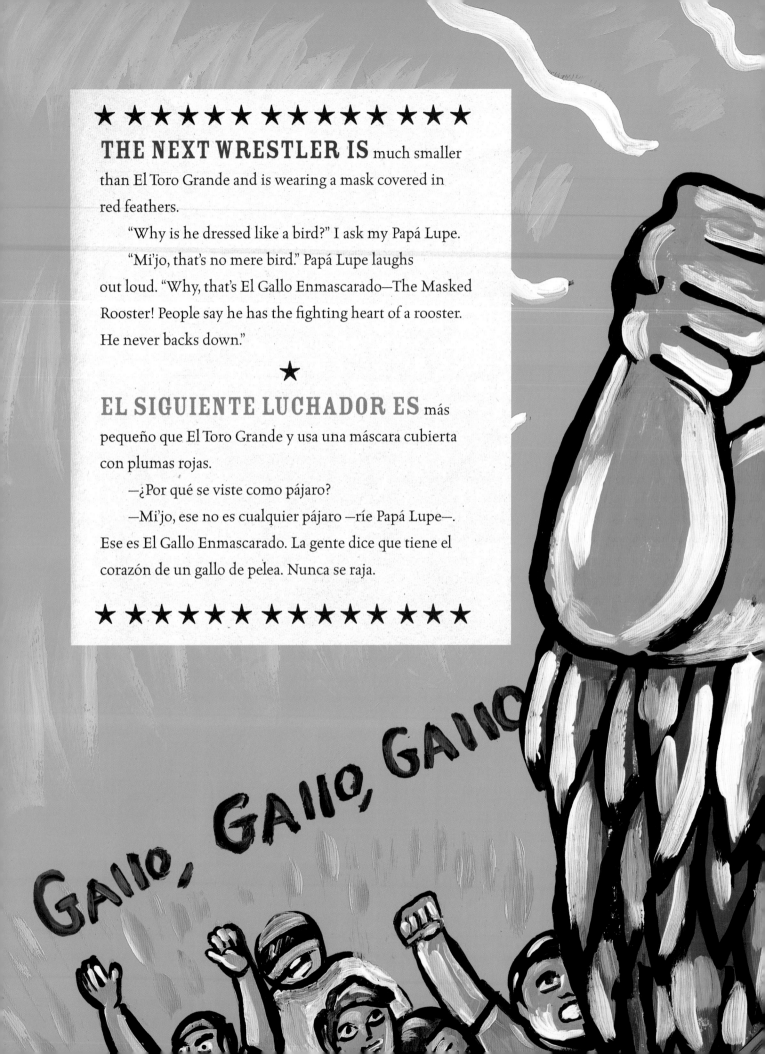

★ ★ ★ ★ ★ ★ ★ ★ ★ ★ ★ ★ ★ ★ ★

THE NEXT WRESTLER IS much smaller than El Toro Grande and is wearing a mask covered in red feathers.

"Why is he dressed like a bird?" I ask my Papá Lupe.

"Mi'jo, that's no mere bird." Papá Lupe laughs out loud. "Why, that's El Gallo Enmascarado—The Masked Rooster! People say he has the fighting heart of a rooster. He never backs down."

★

EL SIGUIENTE LUCHADOR ES más pequeño que El Toro Grande y usa una máscara cubierta con plumas rojas.

—¿Por qué se viste como pájaro?

—Mi'jo, ese no es cualquier pájaro —ríe Papá Lupe—. Ese es El Gallo Enmascarado. La gente dice que tiene el corazón de un gallo de pelea. Nunca se raja.

★ ★ ★ ★ ★ ★ ★ ★ ★ ★ ★ ★ ★ ★ ★

Gallo, Gallo, Gallo

★ ★ ★ ★ ★ ★ ★ ★ ★ ★ ★ ★ ★ ★ ★ ★

CHANTS OF APPROVAL FILL

the arena when the last luchador begins to make his way down to the ring. He is wearing silver wrestling boots and tights.

"He's wearing my mask!" I cry out.

"Actually, mi'jo, you are wearing his mask—that's The Man in the Silver Mask! He is the greatest masked luchador who has ever lived!"

★ ★ ★ ★ ★ ★ ★ ★ ★ ★ ★ ★ ★ ★ ★ ★

★★★★★★★★★★★★★★★★★

LA ARENA SE LLENA de gritos emocionados cuando el último luchador se acerca al ring. Usa leotardo y botas color plata.

—¡Y trae mi máscara! —grito.

—Más bien es al revés, mi'jo, tú estás usando su máscara. Ese es El Hombre de la Máscara Plateada, el más grande luchador de todos los tiempos.

★★★★★★★★★★★★★★★★★

★ ★ ★ ★ ★ ★ ★ ★ ★ ★ ★ ★ ★ ★

AS THE MAN IN the Silver Mask makes his way down to the ring, he stops for a minute right by where Papá Lupe and I are sitting. His eyes look right at me. Then The Man in the Silver Mask smiles at me as if he knows me!

"Why did he smile at me?" I ask my Papá Lupe.

"Who knows?" says Papá Lupe. "Maybe he thinks you'll be a great luchador one day!"

★

ANTES DE LLEGAR AL ring, El Hombre de la Máscara Plateada se detiene un momento junto a donde Papá Lupe y yo estamos sentados. Puedo ver sus ojos mirándome. ¡El Hombre de la Máscara Plateada sonríe como si me conociera!

—¿Por qué me sonrió? —le pregunto a Papá Lupe.

—Sepa —me dice—. A lo mejor piensa que algún día tú serás también un gran luchador.

★ ★ ★ ★ ★ ★ ★ ★ ★ ★ ★ ★ ★ ★

★ ★ ★ ★ ★ ★ ★ ★ ★ ★ ★ ★ ★ ★ ★ ★ ★ ★ ★

PAPÁ LUPE LIFTS ME up and places me on his shoulders so that I can get a better view.

I watch as The Man in the Silver Mask and his allies are jumped from behind even before the match begins. Los rudos are using every dirty trick in the book to try and steal a tainted victory.

"That's not fair," I cry out, but right away los técnicos start fighting back. The Mighty Bull engages in a test of strength with The Evil Caveman to see who is truly the strongest of the two. The Masked Rooster applies a vise-like headlock to El Cucuy who howls in pain.

"Too bad Tío Vicente isn't here," I tell Papá Lupe.

★ ★ ★ ★ ★ ★ ★ ★ ★ ★ ★ ★ ★ ★ ★ ★ ★ ★ ★

★ ★ ★ ★ ★ ★ ★ ★ ★ ★ ★ ★ ★ ★

PAPÁ LUPE ME LEVANTA y me pone en sus hombros para que yo pueda ver mejor.

Veo cómo sorprenden a El Hombre de la Máscara Plateada y a sus aliados. Los atacan por atrás antes de que empiece la lucha. Los rudos usan todas las trampas posibles para poder ganar.

—No se vale —grito, pero rápido los técnicos empiezan a defenderse. El Toro Grande se enfrenta a El Cavernícola para ver quién es el más fuerte de los dos. El Gallo Enmascarado le aplica un candado en la cabeza a El Cucuy que se queja, adolorido.

—Lástima que mi tío Vicente no está aquí —le digo a Papá Lupe.

★ ★ ★ ★ ★ ★ ★ ★ ★ ★ ★ ★ ★ ★

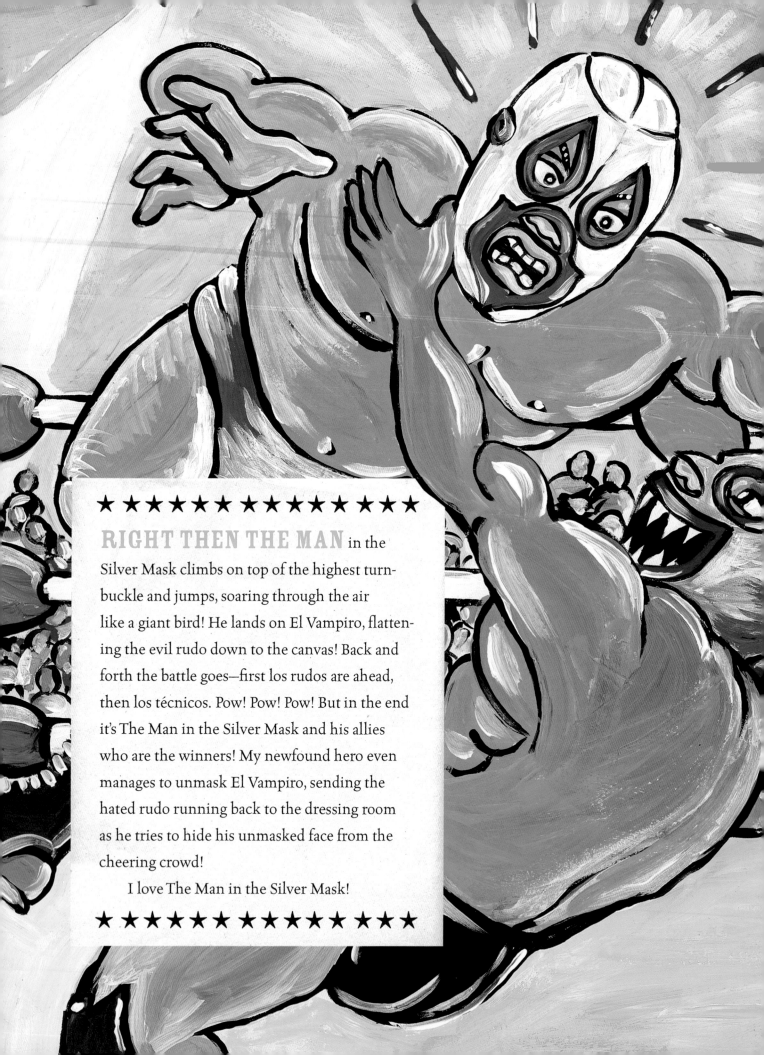

★ ★ ★ ★ ★ ★ ★ ★ ★ ★ ★ ★ ★ ★ ★ ★ ★ ★

RIGHT THEN THE MAN in the
Silver Mask climbs on top of the highest turn-
buckle and jumps, soaring through the air
like a giant bird! He lands on El Vampiro, flatten-
ing the evil rudo down to the canvas! Back and
forth the battle goes—first los rudos are ahead,
then los técnicos. Pow! Pow! Pow! But in the end
it's The Man in the Silver Mask and his allies
who are the winners! My newfound hero even
manages to unmask El Vampiro, sending the
hated rudo running back to the dressing room
as he tries to hide his unmasked face from the
cheering crowd!

I love The Man in the Silver Mask!

★ ★ ★ ★ ★ ★ ★ ★ ★ ★ ★ ★ ★ ★ ★ ★ ★ ★

★ ★ ★ ★ ★ ★ ★ ★ ★ ★ ★ ★ ★ ★ ★ ★ ★ ★

ENTONCES EL HOMBRE DE

la Máscara Plateada se sube a la cuerda más alta y brinca, cruzando el aire como un enorme pájaro. Cae arriba de El Vampiro, aplastando al rudo sobre la lona. Y así sigue la batalla, primero los rudos van ganando, luego los técnicos. ¡Pum! ¡Pum! ¡Pum! Pero al final son El Hombre de la Máscara Plateada y sus aliados quienes ganan la lucha. Mi nuevo héroe incluso logra quitarle la máscara a El Vampiro, haciendo que el rudo se vaya corriendo a los camerinos, tapándose la cara con las manos entre la gente emocionada.

    ¡Me encanta El Hombre de la Máscara Plateada!

★ ★ ★ ★ ★ ★ ★ ★ ★ ★ ★

I'M SAD IT'S OVER, but when we go outside, I am really surprised to find my uncle waiting there. "Tio Vicente!" I cry out. "How did you get here?"

"Oh, it's a long story. Look, I brought something for you," says Tio Vicente. He hands me a silver-masked wrestling figure.

"Wow, this is for me?"

★

ME PONGO TRISTE PORQUE se acaba; pero cuando salimos me sorprende encontrar a mi tío esperándonos.

—¡Tío Vicente! —le grito—. ¿¡Cómo llegaste aquí!?

—Es una larga historia. Pero mira, te traje un regalo —dijo mi tío Vicente. Era un pequeño luchador de plástico con la máscara plateada.

—Órale ¿es para mí?

★ ★ ★ ★ ★ ★ ★ ★ ★ ★ ★ ★ ★ ★ ★ ★

ON THE RIDE HOME, Tío Vicente laughs every time he hears me talk of how great The Man in the Silver Mask was. Maybe he doesn't believe me.

"He could have easily beaten all of the three rudos by himself, he is that good!" I assure him.

Then I notice the strange way that my Tío Vicente and Papá Lupe smile at each other. For a minute, I wonder if they know something about The Man in the Silver Mask that I don't know, but then I stop thinking about them because I just want to think about the famous luchador who is now my greatest hero!

Maybe one day...I can be just like him.

★ ★ ★ ★ ★ ★ ★ ★ ★ ★ ★ ★ ★ ★ ★ ★

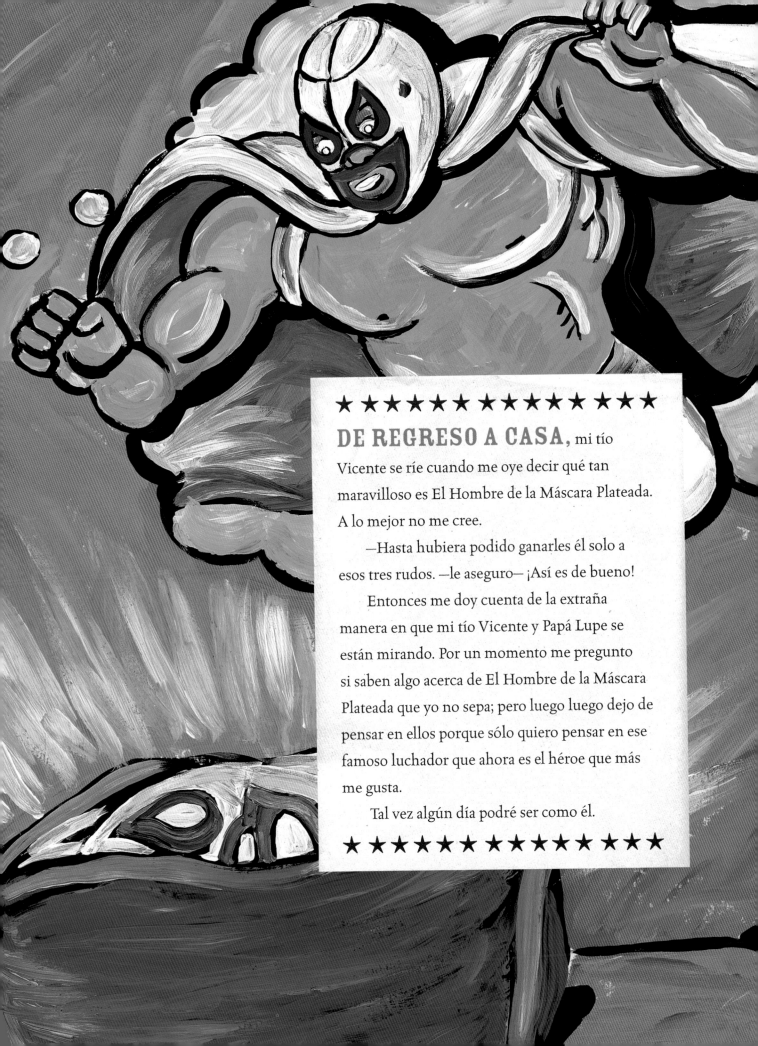

★ ★ ★ ★ ★ ★ ★ ★ ★ ★ ★ ★ ★ ★ ★ ★ ★

DE REGRESO A CASA, mi tío
Vicente se ríe cuando me oye decir qué tan
maravilloso es El Hombre de la Máscara Plateada.
A lo mejor no me cree.

—Hasta hubiera podido ganarles él solo a
esos tres rudos. —le aseguro— ¡Así es de bueno!

Entonces me doy cuenta de la extraña
manera en que mi tío Vicente y Papá Lupe se
están mirando. Por un momento me pregunto
si saben algo acerca de El Hombre de la Máscara
Plateada que yo no sepa; pero luego luego dejo de
pensar en ellos porque sólo quiero pensar en ese
famoso luchador que ahora es el héroe que más
me gusta.

Tal vez algún día podré ser como él.

★ ★ ★ ★ ★ ★ ★ ★ ★ ★ ★ ★ ★ ★ ★ ★ ★

LUCHA LIBRE
A BRIEF BUT TREMENDOUSLY
EXCITING HISTORY

★ ★ ★ ★ ★ ★ ★ ★ ★ ★ ★ ★ ★ ★ ★

EVEN BEFORE EL ENMASCARADO

Nuñez donned a crude black leather hood or La Maravilla Enmascarada—alias Cyclon Mackey—set foot inside a wrestling ring, people have been drawn to the allure of lucha libre and its masked men and women. Fans have come to view the masked wrestlers as symbols of power and mystery.

In Mexico, lucha libre is the poor man's theater. For the price of a few pesos, the common man can treat his family to an incredible world filled with heroes and villains cast in leading and supporting roles. In lucha libre, individuals express themselves artistically, using their very own bodies and person-alities as a canvas of sorts. They put on colorful—at times outrageous—costumes which enable them to become saints, devils, Aztec deities and other outland-ish personalities. They touch upon our childhood fears, taking us back to a more innocent time when we believed that such creatures as vampires and werewolves actually walked the earth. They become defenders of all that is good, personifying even

wrestling priests who preach the word of God even as they are dispensing divine justice with a clenched fist!

Lucha libre and its roots in Mexico can be traced back to the visionary efforts of Salvador Lutteroth Gonzalez. After running a successful family furniture business, he began promoting wrestling cards in what was then called La Arena Mexico, one of the first and most historically significant arenas in Mexico's history. The Vince McMahon of his day, Lutteroth revolutionized the sport of lucha libre, turning what was once viewed as a mere side show into a spectacular extravaganza that depicted the constant struggle of good versus evil. Combining the visual with the dramatic, he created El Murcielago Velasquez (The Bat Velasquez), the first Mexican wrestler to ever wear a mask. Dressing him in a black hood with cutout sil-houettes for his eyes, the vampire cape-wearing villain was a truly frightening sight. Unable to see anything but his eyes, lucha libre fans found themselves irresist-ibly drawn to this mysterious figure.

Who was he? Where did he come from?

El Murciélago Velasquez, while a unique commodity at the time, wouldn't be alone for long. Having captured the imagination of the lucha-libre-going public, Lutteroth followed up with adversaries who would do battle against this evil, masked ruffian. It was under Lutteroth's watchful eyes that such legendary heroes and villains as The White Angel, The Blue Demon, The Red Devil, Mil Mascaras and Jalisco Lightning first came into being. And with Lutteroth as mentor, a young man named Rodolfo Guzmán Huerta would go on to become the biggest lucha libre icon that the world has ever known.

HE WORE A SILVER MASK

In Mexico, the term "tener angel" is used to identify a person who has that special something which marks him out for greatness. Rodolfo Guzmán Huerta had "angel." Just as Salvador Lutteroth Gonzalez revolutionized the sport of lucha libre, so the character created by Rodolfo Guzman Huerta revolutionized the way luchadores were perceived by the general public. The character that fans came to know as Santo, El Enmascarado de Plata became firmly embedded in Mexican popular culture.

El Santo made his start on July 26, 1942. During a 51-year career, he defeated countless opponents, unmasking many of the greatest luchadores in lucha libre history. In 1951, nine years after his in-ring debut, El Santo became the principal character in a series of comic books that bore his name and image. It was because of these comic books that "Santo, the defender of the people" was born. Seven years later, the vast popularity of the Santo comics led their protagonist into another form of expression—Santo

contra El Cerebro del Mal ("Santo versus The Evil Brain"), and Santo contra Los Infernales ("Santo versus The Infernal Men") were among the first films Santo made in a movie career that spanned over 54 films.

As a movie star, El Santo reached iconic status in Mexico, winning the hearts of millions. Today, these films are viewed as cult classic b-films which captured both the innocence and foolishness of an era. Fans would rush to theaters to see Rodolfo Guzman Huerta don his famed silver mask so he could wage war against the forces of evil in its many shapes and forms. Werewolves, evil scientists, vampire women or invaders from the planet Mars—El Santo put them all down in defeat as his fans watched from the safety of their seats. Through these films, El Santo helped to give birth to a genre of lucha libre movies that formed a crucial part of the golden age of Mexican cinema.

El Santo's life came to an abrupt end in 1984. His doctor told him that he was suffering from a severe heart condition that was both incurable and untreatable. Ever the showman and knowing that his days were numbered, El Santo asked to be interviewed live on national television. During these interviews, he publicly unmasked himself, revealing to all of Mexico a secret identity and face he had protected for over 50 years. Only a few days later, he suffered a heart attack, fulfilling prophesies that were often made in his movies—El Santo without his mask would become a mere mortal like everybody else. El Santo's funeral was televised and was open to the general public. Rodolfo Guzmán Huerta, the man who was El Santo in life, was laid to rest wearing his famed silver mask.

DEDICATED TO MY WIFE IRMA AND MY SON VINCENT AND TO EACH AND
EVERY LUCHA LIBRE FAN OUT THERE. —XAVIER GARZA

FIRST EDITION

10 9 8 7 6 5

Library of Congress Cataloging-in-Publication Data

Garza, Xavier.
 Lucha libre : the Man in the Silver Mask : a bilingual cuento / by Xavier Garza.-- 1st ed.
  p. cm.
 Summary: When Carlitos attends a wrestling match in Mexico City with his father, his favorite masked-wrestler has eyes that are strangely familiar.
 ISBN-13: 978-1-933693-10-1; ISBN-10: 933693-10-X (alk. paper)
[1. Uncles—Fiction. 2. Heroes—Fiction. 3. Wrestling—Fiction. 4. Mexico City (Mexico)—Fiction. 5. Spanish language materials—Bilingual.] I. Title.
 PZ73.G27 2005
 [Fic]—dc22

2004029756

BOOK AND COVER DESIGN BY ANTONIO CASTRO H.

Thanks to Luis Humberto Crosthwaite, Sharon Franco, Joe Hayes and Karen Arneson
—los técnicos for sure.